KATHI APPELT

The Alley Cat's

Meow

ILLUSTRATED BY

JON GOODELL

HARCOURT, INC.   San Diego New York London

Library of Congress Cataloging-in-Publication Data
Appelt, Kathi, 1954–
The Alley Cat's Meow/Kathi Appelt; illustrated by Jon Goodell.
p. cm.
Summary: After meeting one night at the Alley Cat's Meow, sweetheart cats
Red and Ginger dazzle the world with their spectacular dancing.
[1. Cats—Fiction.   2. Dance—Fiction.   3. Stories in rhyme.]
I. Goodell, Jon, ill.   II. Title.
PZ8.3.A554Al   2002
[E]—dc21   2001005966
ISBN 0-15-201980-4

First edition
H G F E D C B A

Printed in Singapore

The illustrations in this book were painted in oil and acrylic on acrylic-primed linen canvas.
The display lettering was created by Jane Dill, based on Jon Goodell's illustration.
The text type was set in Belucian Book.
Color separations by Bright Arts Ltd., Hong Kong
Printed and bound by Tien Wah Press, Singapore
This book was printed on totally chlorine-free Nymolla Matte Art paper.
Production supervision by Sandra Grebenar and Pascha Gerlinger
Designed by Linda Lockowitz

To Betsy and Kevin—two cool cats—with love!
—K. A.

To true love, and my mom and dad,
the first people who loved me
—J. G.

It was a full moon, jazz tune,
swingin' kind of night,
when Red hopped on the A train
and it rumbled out of sight.

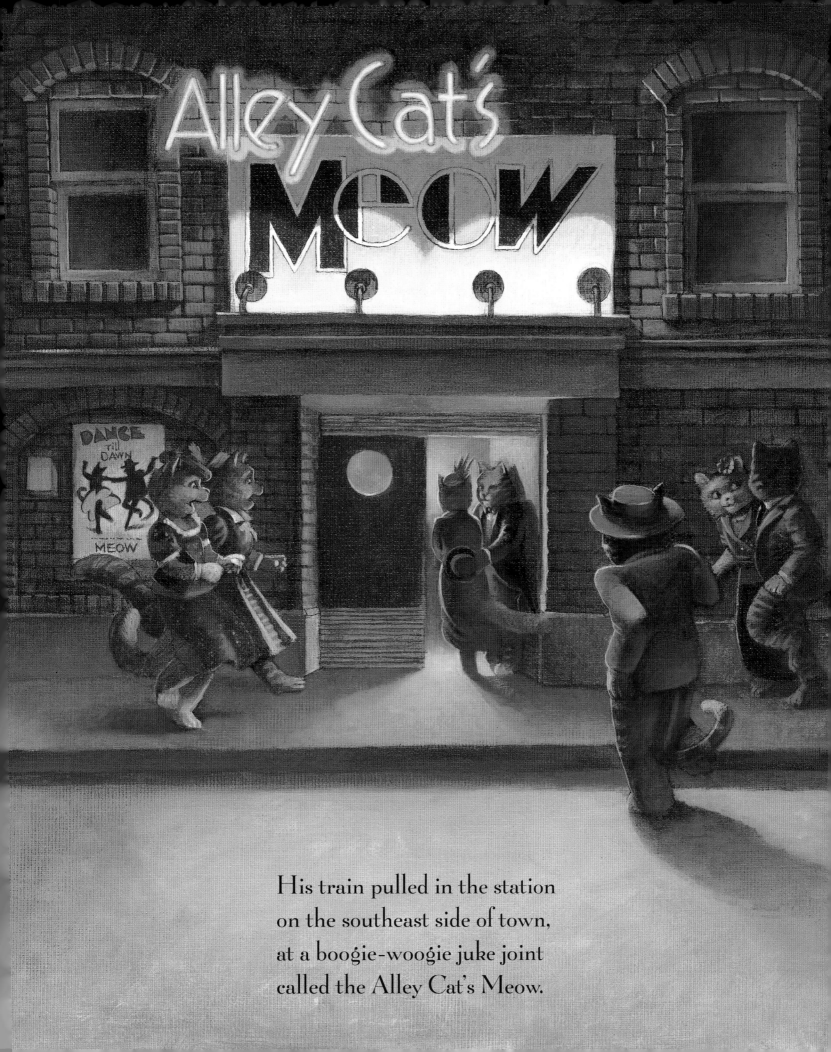

His train pulled in the station
on the southeast side of town,
at a boogie-woogie juke joint
called the Alley Cat's Meow.

He straightened out his whiskers
and smoothed his coat of silk,
then found a little table
and signaled for a milk.

On the other side of Alleytown,
Miss Ginger stepped upon
the Catanooga Choo-Choo,
then it chug-a-lugged along.

The show was just beginning
as she mingled with the crowd.
Red's toes, they started tingling
as toward him Ginger prowled.

She was jazzy, she was snazzy,
she was *my oh my oh my.*

He cocked his ear and hoped
that he could catch her hazel eye.

He'd never seen another
quite as luminous as her.
He rose and kissed her outstretched paw,
then couldn't help it—purred.

"Oh my!" Miss Ginger started....

He was dashing, he was smashing,
he was *la di da di da*.
When he asked her if she'd care to dance,
her heart went *cha-cha-cha*.

They jitterbugged and cut a rug.

They did the waltz and samba.

Their cat-trot was exceptional.
Magnificent! *¡Caramba!*

Miss Ginger gave a curtsy.
Red doffed his hat and bowed.

Then he swooped her up and kissed her—
the audience was wowed!

and across the silver screen.

They high-kicked in Las Vegas

and cancanned in Paree.

They tapped in old Havana—

in Brazil, the tarantella.
Oh, how Red loved Miss Ginger...
and Ginger loved her fella.

For every time he took her paws,
her heart, it pitter-pattered,
and when she purred into his ears,
her love was all that mattered.

So if you take the A train,
or the Catanooga line,
remember Red and Ginger
when the moon is full of shine.

There's a boogie-woogie juke joint
on the southeast side of town....
You might catch them, if you're lucky,
at the Alley Cat's Meow.